TEN WEEKS TO TARGET

Divorcee Janine has outgrown her entire wardrobe. Her niece's wedding is in ten weeks. Drastic action is needed. She joins a slimming club where she meets Pete, whose wife has given him an ultimatum: 'Lose four stone or I'm leaving you' . . . The two support each other through the dramas of life, as well as slimming, but reaching their targets turns out to be a new beginning — in more ways than one.

Books by Della Galton
in the Linford Romance Library:

NEVER LET GO
SHADOWMAN

DELLA GALTON

TEN WEEKS TO TARGET

Complete and Unabridged

LINFORD
Leicester

First published in Great Britain in 2005

First Linford Edition
published 2012

British Library CIP Data

Galton, Della.
  Ten weeks to target. - -
  (Linford romance library)
  1. Love stories.
  2. Large type books.
  I. Title II. Series
  823.9'2–dc23

  ISBN 978–1–4448–0991–6

Published by
F. A. Thorpe (Publishing)
Anstey, Leicestershire

Set by Words & Graphics Ltd.
Anstey, Leicestershire
Printed and bound in Great Britain by
T. J. International Ltd., Padstow, Cornwall

This book is printed on acid-free paper

1

'Why don't you just get a bigger size, Mum?'

'Very good question,' Janine thought, as she struggled to get the zip done up on her jeans. Everything was so simple when you were fourteen going on twenty-five and could eat whatever you wanted without putting on a pound. She glanced at Kelly, who was sitting on the bed, her dark hair gelled into hedgehog spikes and her blue eyes impatient.

'Because I don't want a bigger size,' she said patiently. 'I want to fit into this size.' 'Especially as your Aunt Alison will be looking like she's just stepped off a catwalk,' she could have added.

Alison was her sister-in-law. Alison was perfect. Well, she was in the looks department anyway. She had the sort of cheekbones photographers raved about,

1

not a trace of a laughter line despite being in her mid-forties, blonde hair that always looked effortlessly styled and — most enviably of all in Janine's book right now — she was a size ten.

'If you're getting all done up for Aunt Ali's benefit then I shouldn't bother,' Kelly went on with irritating perception. 'She's far more interested in discussing the wedding of the year than in what you look like.'

'Yes, but that isn't the point,' Janine said, forcing the button into place. It would be all right if she didn't sit down. And if she wore a long top, then maybe she could leave the button undone. With a bit of luck, Ali would be in too much of a rush to stop for long.

'What do you think?' she said, spinning round in front of her daughter. 'Do I look fat?'

'No-oo,' Kelly said, spinning out the O in the way she did when she was trying to think of something diplomatic to say. 'But you do look — er — uncomfortable.'

Uncomfortable was the understatement of the year. And then the doorbell rang and it was suddenly too late. She checked her hair in the mirror. Her shoulder-length brown frizz was in dire need of a cut and grey was coming through at the sides. Why did it always have to come through just at the wrong time?

'Shall I let her in?' Kelly asked, standing up in one careless, graceful movement.

'Yes. No, I'll do it.' Janine reached for her scent — at least she'd smell nice — but, as she stretched forward, her jeans finally gave up the battle and tore along the crotch.

'I'll let Aunt Ali in,' Kelly said calmly and disappeared.

Janine ripped off the ruined jeans and rifled frantically through her wardrobe. No black trousers. Suddenly remembering they were in the wash, she tore into the bathroom and found them screwed up in the bottom of the linen basket.

It would have to be her tracksuit bottoms. She hauled them off the hanger, remembering belatedly that the last time she'd worn them had been to emulsion the spare room, which wasn't quite finished. They were paint-spattered, but at least they fitted. She raced across the landing and put her head round the spare-room door. A tray of paintbrushes was laid out neatly on some newspaper. She grabbed one and went downstairs slowly.

Alison and Kelly were sitting at the kitchen table, bent over a wedding magazine. Janine put on her brightest smile.

'Hi, Ali. Sorry, I forgot you were coming. I was just — er — doing a bit of decorating.' With a bit of luck she could pass off the grey in her hair as paint.

'Oh, don't let me stop you.' Alison glanced up. She looked breathtaking, as usual, in a navy and white suit. Positively nautical, Janine thought, which was per-haps why she felt a bit sick. Or perhaps that was because she was afraid that Kelly would give the game away and she'd have to confess that she had simply outgrown her wardrobe. All of it, without even noticing.

But all her darling daughter did was to raise her eyebrows and shake her head slightly. 'I'll put the kettle on while you two talk weddings,' she said, sliding off her chair and coming across the kitchen. She took the dry paintbrush out of Janine's hand. 'And I'll put this in some white spirit, shall I, Mum? Save it going all stiff and hard.'

Fortunately, Alison didn't seem too interested in the decorating. 'I thought you'd like to see the place cards we finally decided on,' she murmured, barely glancing at Janine. 'Gorgeous, aren't they?'

'Lovely,' Janine agreed, looking at the pink-and-blue-edged cards.

'They'll go in gold place-holders,' Alison went on. 'Mia thought you might like to see the seating layout, too. You're going to be here.' She pointed a pale pink fingernail. 'Next to Mia's Uncle Martin. Remember him? He's just split up with his wife, too. Poor man was devastated.'

Great, Janine thought. A table of discarded aunts and uncles, neatly packaged away by the fire exit by the look of it.

'It'll cheer him up sitting with you,' Alison went on brightly. 'Have you decided what you're going to wear yet?'

'I haven't had much time to think about it. What with the decorating.'

'Well, chop chop, it's only ten weeks away now, you know. I've had my outfit for a year.'

Janine nodded miserably and resisted the urge to confess that if she'd had her outfit for a year, she'd have had to let it out by at least three sizes by now. Some women gave up eating when they were unhappy, but unfortunately she'd never been one of them. Since she and Jonathan had separated she'd piled on weight like there was no tomorrow. Well, chocolate was so much more comforting than salad, wasn't it? But she felt quite unable to say any of this to Alison, who actually looked as if she'd lost weight lately.

'Mind you, I'll have to get it taken in,' Alison muttered, flapping the waistband of her skirt. 'What with all this running about, I'm losing weight by the bucket-load. Anyway, Janine, dear, I'll leave you to your decorating. You're obviously up to your eyes in it. And, don't take this the wrong way, will you, but . . . ' She hesitated. 'I thought you might like to get your hair done before the wedding at my salon. My treat, of course.'

'That's very sweet of you,' Janine said through gritted teeth.

'I'll see myself out,' Alison trilled, gathering up her place settings and slipping them into her slimline designer handbag.

'She means well,' Kelly said, reading her mother's face as they came back into the kitchen. 'And you'll look great whatever you wear.'

7

'Thank you, darling.' She treated her daughter to a hug, breathing in the mix of hair gel and apple shampoo and feeling a mixture of despair that she was a fat and frumpy forty-year-old and relief that she had such a gorgeous, sweet daughter. 'But we both know that's not true. Anyway, at least one of us will look beautiful.'

'Mia's too young to get married,' Kelly went on blithely. 'I'm never getting married. Especially not to a dork like Carl Baker — I don't know what she sees in him.'

Janine frowned. Privately, she agreed that nineteen was very young to take such a big step, but then Mia had always been mature for her age. She was a lovely girl, shy and sensible. She'd seen a lot of her when she was younger, but they'd hardly spoken lately. Poor Mia was probably rushed off her feet with wedding plans.

'I expect she loves him,' she told Kelly. 'That's the usual reason to get married, isn't it?'

8

'Didn't help much with you and Dad, did it?'

Ouch, Janine thought, changing her mind about Kelly being gorgeous and sweet. Mentions of her ex-husband still hurt far more than she wanted to admit. She wasn't looking forward to seeing him at the wedding with his new girl-friend, who was thin, naturally.

God, she was going to have to lose some weight before then. Perhaps she could get a padlock for the biscuit tin and the fridge, and she could have a ceremonial burning of all the take-away menus in the house.

They were on their way to school the next day when Kelly said hesitantly, 'You could always try a slimming club. Sharon Smith's mum lost three stone at hers.'

'Bet it took more than ten weeks,' Janine muttered, slowing for a red light.

'Yes, but you don't need to lose three stone. A stone wouldn't take long, would it?'

'I'm not a slimming club type of

person, though, darling. I can't think of anything worse than sitting in a room with a load of women discussing diets.'

'It's not just women who go these days. There are three men in Sharon's mum's group.'

'That sounds even worse,' Janine said, and then felt guilty at her daughter's pained expression. 'All right, I'll think about it,' she said, as they pulled up at the school gates. 'Have a good day, pet.'

She still wasn't quite sure how on earth she'd let herself be talked into it when she walked into the 'New You' Slimming Club the following Tuesday evening. As she stood at the end of a queue of chattering women she very nearly lost her nerve and ran. It was only the fact that she'd promised Kelly that stopped her. The class was being held at a primary school about two miles from where she lived, and there was a board at the entrance that said, *Come on in — you have nothing to lose but weight.*

She could think of a lot of other things she had to lose. Dignity being the main one. The last time she'd been to a slimming club, the group leader had thought it motivating to tell everyone in the room how much you weighed. Mind you, that had been several years ago. She closed her eyes and prayed things had changed.

* * *

Pete Carter was, if anything, feeling even more out of place than Janine. He was two places in front of her in the queue. He wouldn't have been here at all if he hadn't been desperate.

'Lose four stone, or you lose me. It's a simple choice. I'm sick of being married to a fat slob.'

Sarah's cruel words had lodged like bullets in his heart. She'd never complained about his weight before. He'd always been big. He was six foot four; he'd have looked silly if he was thin. Not that he could be described as thin by any stretch of the imagination, he thought. But she'd never seemed to mind before. She'd always said he'd made her feel safe, protected. When had that changed?

If he thought about it, he could track it back to the time she'd started her new secretarial job. Or, to be more precise, the first time they'd gone out on a social with her new workmates. They'd gone to one of those carvery places, the type where you can eat as much as you like. He'd been busily piling roast potatoes on to his plate when she'd nudged him sharply. 'Haven't you got enough there, Pete? Leave some for everyone else.' A jokey little comment; apart from the fact that her eyes had said she'd meant it.

Well, other than putting some of the potatoes back again, which seemed a bit embarrassing, he couldn't do anything about it. But, ever since then, she'd been making snide remarks about his weight. And then, last week, when they'd had dinner with her parents, things had come to a head. He didn't want to think about last week, it was too humiliating.

He blinked, aware that the woman at the desk was speaking to him.

'First time is it, dear?'

He nodded, aware of her curious eyes, knowing he was flushing scarlet.

'Take this form over to the table in the corner. Colette will be over to sort you out shortly. Then you can get yourself weighed in.'

'Oh joy,' Pete thought. He shuffled over to the corner table. There was still time to escape. He thought of Sarah and decided to stay put.

A few moments later, he glanced up to see a pretty, dark-haired woman heading towards him.

'Are you Colette?'

'No, I'm Janine. It's my first time, too.' She looked as nervous as he was.

'You're not here to lose weight, though, surely. There's nothing of you.'

She smiled. She was even prettier when she smiled. It lit up her grey-blue eyes. 'What a sweet thing to say. But yes, I am, I'm going to my niece's wedding and the rest of my family are like stick insects.'

'Creepy things, stick insects,' he said, warming to her. 'Don't lose too much, will you?'

Before either of them could say anything else they were joined by Colette, and the next ten minutes were spent going through the programme. 'It's not a diet, it's a healthy eating programme.' If she said it once she said it a dozen times.

It certainly looked like a diet to Pete. Unlimited vegetables — preferably raw ones — weren't exactly comfort food, were they?

'Do we — er — get any sort of chocolate allowance?' he asked, when Colette finally paused to draw breath.

'A small bar once a week or so shouldn't hurt.'

Pete felt his hopes plummeting. Janine looked disappointed, too.

'Nothing tastes as good as thin,'

Colette added firmly. 'In a few weeks you'll be agreeing with me.'

Pete was tempted to argue about that, but Colette had a steely glint in her blue eyes that reminded him fleetingly of Sarah so he didn't. The class wasn't as bad as he'd feared. It had been a shock to find out just how much he actually weighed. But at least they'd done the dirty deed in private. Only the woman doing the weighing, who wrote it down on their cards, actually knew exactly how bad things were. He'd watched her carefully for sarcastic eyebrow-raising, but she'd kept her face blank. Obviously a professional actress. It was also helped by the fact that he'd sat next to Janine. He wondered if her husband approved of her coming. He was probably one of these bodybuilder types, all lithe and muscled.

He clapped dutifully, along with everyone else, every time someone's weight loss was read out. They all seemed to have done very well. He imagined himself coming in next week and being clapped. How much could he reasonably be expected to lose? Quite a bit, judging by the comments flying about.

* * *

'Four pounds off, Pete. That's a great achievement. Well done.'

He felt himself blushing. 'Thanks. Thanks very much.' He settled carefully on the seat beside Janine. 'How did you do?'

'Three pounds.' She beamed at him proudly. 'Not so bad, is it? I missed my chocolate, though.'

'Me too. Ah well, it won't be for ever.'

'Are you dieting for a special occasion?' she asked.

He shook his head, knowing he could never tell her that he was dieting to save his marriage. To stop his beautiful Sarah from feeling ashamed of him, to be able to hold his head up high next time he visited his in-laws. They might even have forgotten about their broken dining-room chair by then.

'Lucky you,' she said. 'I'm on a deadline. I've got nine weeks to fit into my wedding outfit.'

'Couldn't you just buy a bigger size?'

'That's what my daughter said.' She smiled ruefully. 'To be honest, I'm only here because of her. Have you got kids?'

'Nah. My wife's too into her career at the moment. Maybe some time in the future, though.'

* * *

Janine had been dieting for three weeks when Mia popped round.

'Mum said to let you know she's booked a preliminary appointment for your hair consultation,' she said, getting a card out of her bag. 'Three-fifteen on Saturday, if that's OK?'

She looked a bit fraught, Janine noticed. Her pretty face was strained and she had dark shadows under her eyes. 'So, how's it all going?' she asked gently. 'Are you looking forward to your big day?'

'There's a part of me that will be glad when it's all over,' Mia said with a nervous little smile.

'It's an awful lot to organise, isn't it?'

'Mum's doing most of the organising,' Mia mumbled, not meeting her eyes.

'Well, if ever you want to escape from wedding talk you're always welcome to come by. I know these things can get on top of you.'

'Thanks.'

For a moment, Janine thought she was going to say something else, but she just sighed, said she was late for a dress fitting and fled.

Janine closed the door thoughtfully behind her. Mia wasn't her usual, cheerful self at all. Perhaps she ought to have a word with her brother, Nick, but she didn't want to rock the boat. Besides, there was a distinct possibility that she was imagining things. Living on a diet of raw vegetables might be wonderful for her figure, but she didn't think it was doing much for her concentration. Mia wasn't the only one who'd be glad when the wedding day was over, she thought ruefully. It was worth it, though, on week four, when she got her half-stone award, a little gold sticker to put in her weight record book.

'Teacher's pet,' Pete whispered as she sat back beside him. But there was warmth in his dark brown eyes. She smiled at him. He was a nice man, uncomplicated and genuine.

'I've existed mostly on raw carrots this week,' she confessed; as they filed out of the class afterwards. 'I don't know how much longer I can keep this up.'

'At this rate you won't have to keep it up much longer. You're halfway there, aren't you?'

Inspired by his words, she nipped into the supermarket on the way home and filled up her trolley with healthy food. She was just sailing past the cake aisle, her eyes averted as she tried not to breathe in the tantalising scent of

Danish pastries, her favourite, when she narrowly missed a trolley coming in the opposite direction.

'Sorry — oh, hello, Pete. Stocking up?'

'Er, yes — you?'

He looked stricken, she saw, and, as her gaze dropped to his trolley, she could see why. He'd got a whole stack of marked-down cake boxes piled up at one end of it, supported by several four-packs of lager, with a family-size bar of chocolate balanced across the top of them. In one corner of his trolley, looking as out of place as a teetotaller in a beer tent, were a couple of bottles of diet cola.

'Tut, tut,' she said playfully. 'If Colette could see you now.'

'You're not going to tell her, are you?' Pete said miserably.

'I won't need to, will I? The scales will do that when you get on them next week. It seems a shame when you're doing so well.'

'I don't think I'm cut out for dieting.'

He looked so crestfallen that Janine almost wished she hadn't caught him. She passed him at the checkout with what looked like a family-size pack of salad on top of the cake boxes. Camouflage, perhaps, in case he bumped into anyone else from slimming club, or did he think the salad was going to somehow counteract the rest of his supplies?

She queued up, trying to ignore the bars of chocolate calling to her from beside the checkout. She managed it, but instead of being pleased with herself, she drove home feeling curiously deflated. It was Pete's fault, she decided. He'd become an ally over the last few weeks. They'd even swapped mobile-phone numbers, so they could talk each other out of making any rash food decisions they'd later regret. Not that they'd ever actually phoned each other. But it had been the two of them against temptation and he'd caved in already. Silly, really, to be disappointed when she hardly knew the man, but she was. She was at home unpacking her supplies when the doorbell rang. To her surprise, she found Mia on her doorstep.

'Hello, love, I didn't know you were coming round tonight. Was it more wedding arrangements?'

'Sort of,' Mia began and then her voice cracked. 'Oh, Aunt Janine, something terrible's happened.'

Janine was torn between hugging her and ushering her inside. In the end, she compromised and put her arm around Mia's shoulders and led her sobbing into the kitchen.

★ ★ ★

'Carl doesn't want to go through with the wedding,' Mia whispered, when she'd got through several pieces of kitchen roll.

'But why ever not, pet? I thought you two were so happy.'

Mia blew her nose again noisily and didn't answer this. 'Mum's going to kill me.'

'Of course she isn't. It's not your fault.'

'She is. Everything's booked. And it's been really expensive. And I heard her and Dad arguing about it the other day. They can't really afford such a big do, especially a big do that isn't even going to happen. And they'll still have to pay for it all anyway and, oh my God, what am I going to do?' She burst into tears again and Janine squeezed her hand.

'Mia, darling, listen to me. Your mum loves you and she might be a bit shocked, but she wouldn't want you to marry Carl if you weren't both absolutely sure about it. Anyway, are you positive he doesn't want to go through with it? I know it's brides who are supposed to get pre-wedding jitters, but maybe he's feeling a bit nervous?'

Mia shook her head and Janine went on gently, 'Would you like me to have a word with your parents?'

'No. I'm not that much of a coward. I'll tell them — I don't want to tell them yet, though. Can I stay here tonight?'

'Of course you can. But you'll need to let them know.'

'I won't. They'll assume I'm at Carl's.'

'All right,' Janine said uneasily.

The kitchen door opened and Kelly popped her head round it. 'Oh, hi, Mia, I didn't know you were here. You've got a text, Mum. From someone called Pete. You didn't tell me you were seeing someone.'

'I'm not seeing anyone. And what are you doing reading my texts? You'd go mad if I started reading yours.'

'You left your mobile in the bathroom,' Kelly said irrationally, and then she noticed, belatedly, that Mia was upset. 'Hey, what's up, Mia?'

Mia looked as though she was going to cry again and Janine glared at her daughter and snatched the mobile out of her hand.

The text message was only one word long. It said *HELP*, in capital letters, and was signed *Pete*.

She sighed. Why did everyone want her help at the same time? She was tempted to ignore Pete, but then she thought of him sitting surrounded by cake boxes and texting her in a last, desperate bid to resist them, and she knew she couldn't let him down.

'Make your cousin another coffee,' she told Kelly. 'I just have to phone someone.' She took the phone out into the hall and dialled his number. She'd never understood why people texted each other when it was much quicker to phone.

'It's Janine,' she murmured. 'Responding to your SOS. How can I be of assistance?'

'Oh, hi, Janine. Thanks for calling.' He sounded surprised to hear from her. He also sounded as though he had his mouth full.

'Am I too late?' she asked ruefully.

'No. No, you're not. You're fine. I'm eating salad. I swear.' He crunched something to prove his point. 'I wasn't going to. I was just going to dive straight in and scoff those cakes, but I haven't.'

She smiled. 'What have you done with them?'

'I gave them to my next-door neighbour.'

'And the chocolate?'

'I've still got that. I unwrapped it — and then I texted you. It's sitting in front of me.'

Janine could feel her mouth watering. Chocolate and emergencies had always gone hand in hand. And the drama unfolding in her kitchen definitely counted as an emergency.

'Bin it,' she said firmly. 'Wrap it up again and put it in the wheelie bin right now. I'll wait while you do it.'

She could hear his footsteps going along the hall and then there was a lot of banging about — presumably the front door, followed by the dustbin lid.

'Mission accomplished,' he reported back.

'Great. Well done. No getting it out again when I've gone.'

'I'm not that much of a pig.'

She smiled. 'I'm afraid I've got to go. I'm in the middle of a domestic crisis. See you next week.'

* * *

When she got back into the kitchen, Mia and Kelly were talking earnestly.

'Tell Mum what you just told me,' Kelly said in her bossiest twenty-five-year-old voice. 'Go on, or I'll tell her.'

'Carl called off the wedding because I'm pregnant,' Mia whispered. 'Thirteen weeks. It's probably just as well he called it off. I'm never going to fit into my dress anyway.'

'Ah,' Janine murmured, sitting back at the table. 'But that's not the end of the world, is it? I mean, just because it wasn't planned, it doesn't mean he won't come round to the idea, given a bit of time.'

'It's not that simple,' Mia said, twiddling a strip of kitchen roll round and round her fingers until it fell to pieces and looking up at Janine with tear-washed eyes. 'You see, Auntie Janine, Carl dumped me because he isn't the father.'

2

Janine tried not to let her emotions show on her face as she met Mia's stricken gaze. She just said, 'Ah,' again, and 'I see,' her mind spinning as she tried to absorb this bombshell.

To say she was shocked was an understatement. Carl and Mia had been going out with each other for more than three years. But then she remembered how uneasy Mia had seemed when she'd called round the previous week and how she'd passed it off as pre-wedding nerves. So maybe her instincts hadn't been quite so far out, after all.

She was aware, however, as she looked into her niece's tearstained face, that she ought to tread very carefully here. Absently, she picked up the kitchen roll that Mia had discarded and tore off a piece to twiddle with.

'I suppose you're wondering who the father is?' Mia said, a mixture of defiance and something else that was harder to identify in her voice.

'You don't have to tell me that,' Janine said gently.

'It's a bloke called Paul — she met him at her badminton club,' Kelly supplied helpfully. 'She's in love with him, aren't you, Mia?'

Mia lowered her eyes and nodded.

'And does he feel the same about you?' Janine asked.

'I don't know.' Now Mia looked at her and Janine realised that the other emotion was fear. 'He said he loved me when — well, you know — but I haven't told him about the baby yet.'

'How old is he?'

'Thirty-one.'

Janine felt her fingers clench around the kitchen roll. Oh God, this just got better and better. 'Hmm,' she said, wishing she could think of something constructive to say. Wishing that Mia hadn't decided to tell her all this before she told her own parents, because they were going to be more furious about not being the first to know than they were about their daughter's predicament. No, maybe not. They were going to be pretty furious about that. She tried to imagine how she'd feel if Kelly came in and said she was pregnant by a man twelve years her senior.

'I know it's a big age gap,' Mia went on. 'But we just knew how we felt about each other the minute we met. He's my badminton coach. He said I'm really talented.'

I'll bet he did, Janine thought, having visions of a lecherous old man leering at young girls in short skirts. Not that thirty-one was old, of course, but it was when you compared it to nineteen. It was light years away. She shook her head. It wasn't her place to make judgments. Mia had come to her for help.

'Right,' she said briskly. 'Right, well, the first thing to do is not to worry. Let's just have a bit of a think. Does

Carl know who the father is?'

Mia nodded. 'I had to tell him because he thought it was his best mate and he was all set to go round and punch his lights out.'

Janine decided not to ask why Carl had jumped to that conclusion. Things were complicated enough already. It did make things more difficult, though, because if Carl knew, then he was going to tell his parents and there was every chance they'd go and see Mia's parents, which would be a disaster.

'I really think you need to speak to your mum and dad, darling. This is the sort of thing they should hear from you. How about we go round and see them now, me and you together?'

'I can't face it,' Mia said, shaking her head and reaching for the kitchen roll again. 'Not right this minute. Please don't make me. Can't it wait until tomorrow?'

'I'm not going to make you do anything. OK, we'll leave them out of it for a little while. But a very little while.

Have you been to the doctor?'

'I went this morning.'

'And have you thought about what you want to do?'

'I want to have the baby. I want to live with Paul — I don't mind if he won't marry me. I just want to be with him.'

'Then you really need to speak to him, don't you?'

Mia nodded and rummaged in her bag for her mobile.

'Don't tell him on the phone, will you, love?'

'I'm not that silly. I'll invite him round here. Well, I can't go to him. He lives on the other side of town. I can't afford to get a taxi out there. You don't mind, do you?'

'Of course not,' Janine said wearily, although she couldn't imagine anything worse than having baby-snatcher Paul sitting in her kitchen. She'd just have to hope that Alison and Nick didn't find out where their daughter was and come charging round. There'd be murder at the very least if they bumped into Paul, and there was a very big part of Janine that wouldn't have blamed them. She and Alison might not always see eye to eye, but she was on her sister-in-law's side totally on this one.

'Mia, are you absolutely sure you don't want to go home?' she said again.

'Certain,' Mia said firmly, clamping her mobile to her ear. 'Unless you don't want me here?'

'Of course I want you here. You know that.' Janine gave up. She'd just have to deal with the consequences of this later.

Half an hour ago she'd have said her biggest problem was how she was going to get into her wedding outfit. Now it seemed that there was every chance that she wasn't going to need one. But far from feeling relieved about this, she'd have given anything to turn the clock back. For her niece not to be sitting in her kitchen pouring out her heart while her parents sat at home in blissful ignorance, still making plans, no doubt, for the wedding of the year. She thought briefly of Pete and his frantic SOS text and was glad she'd managed to talk him out of a cake binge. At least she'd helped to ensure that he was having a better day than she was.

★ ★ ★

'You're an absolute pig, Pete Carter — don't think I don't know what you've been up to while I've been away. Jean saw you unloading the car yesterday and she said you had a whole load of cake boxes in your shopping.'

Their neighbour must have blooming good eyesight, Pete thought miserably, feeling himself colouring up beneath his wife's furious diatribe. Either that or the nosy old dragon next door had been lying in wait. She'd never approved of him.

'All right,' he said, holding up his hands in a gesture of defeat. 'I did buy a few cakes when I got the groceries. I had a moment of weakness, OK, but I didn't eat them. I swear.'

Sarah put her hands on her hips and stared at him, her furious blue eyes narrowing suspiciously. 'So what did you do with them?'

'I took them round for the kids at number twenty-three. You can check if you don't believe me.'

'We can't afford to subsidise other people's shopping bills,' Sarah said, but her voice was softer now. 'And you know how much I hate wasting money. Why, Pete? Why did you buy them in the first place?'

'I don't know. I guess I've got no willpower. I'm sorry.' The memory of Janine's friendly, smiling voice on the phone last night flashed through his head. Not that there was any way he could tell Sarah that the motivation he'd needed to get rid of those cakes had come from a fellow dieter. If she found out he'd been speaking to another woman, however innocently, she'd probably divorce him on the spot.

'I'm trying my best to eat healthy food, but it's just not easy.' He moved

35

across to his wife and put his arms around her. 'Especially when you're away. I really missed you.'

'I was only away for a couple of days. And these residential courses are really important to my career, Pete. Surely you don't begrudge me that?'

'Of course I don't. I'm proud of you, you know I am.' For a couple of moments he held her, breathing in the soft, spicy scent she always wore and thinking that he'd just have to try harder because he loved her so much and he'd do anything to keep her. He kissed the back of her neck, not sure if he was imagining it or whether she stiffened slightly beneath his touch.

Then she slipped out of his embrace. 'Get off me, you big lummox. Do me a favour and get my case out of the car. I've got to unpack and I've got to write up a report for work. I've got a million and one things to do.'

Her car was parked on the road outside their house and, as he walked up their drive and past their wheelie bin, he suddenly remembered the family-size bar of chocolate that he'd put in there at Janine's insistence. He'd just have to pray that Sarah didn't take it in her head to check the bin for cake boxes. She was going to blow her top if she found that.

★ ★ ★

'I'm scared, Aunt Janine. Mum's going to absolutely murder me, isn't she?'

'Of course she isn't, love,' Janine murmured, although she wasn't at all sure about this. It was just under fourteen hours since Mia had turned up on her doorstep. Mia had tried to get hold of Paul several times last night. She'd left increasingly tearful messages on both his mobile and his home phone, but he still hadn't called her back.

Which made him a rat of the highest order, Janine thought, although she hadn't voiced these thoughts to Mia. 'Perhaps he's away or something,' she'd told her niece. 'I'm sure he'd get back to you if he'd got your messages.'

'Or perhaps he's married,' Kelly had muttered, but fortunately not in front of her cousin.

'Don't you dare let Mia hear you say that,' Janine had said, even though precisely the same thought had occurred to her. 'Poor, poor Mia. What an awful mess to get into.'

And now it was Wednesday morning and they were on their way to Mia's parents. Well, at least, Mia and Janine were. Much to Kelly's disgust, Janine had dropped her off at school first. Janine sighed inwardly. She'd have much rather been sorting out people's insurance claims than on her way to face Alison. They'd been related by marriage for over twenty years, but they'd never done much more than scrape the surface when it came to friendship. When Janine had split up with Jonathan, Alison had phoned and asked how she was, but Janine had sensed that she hadn't really wanted to know the answer. This had been confirmed when she'd told her sister-in-law she'd thrown all Jonathan's clothes out of the window and that it had helped to get it out of her system. Alison had laughed nervously and said that she hoped none of the neighbours had been watching.

'I don't give a damn if they were,' Janine had snapped, but she'd regretted it instantly when she'd heard the sharp, in-drawn breath, and Alison hadn't mentioned Jonathan again.

There wasn't a lot of room for out of control emotion in Alison's life, Janine had thought wryly. Not rage, not grief and probably not even mad excitement. She liked everything in tight, manageable boxes. Neat and organised and predictable. Mia's news was going to be one heck of a shock.

She glanced at her niece, who had her hands clenched in her lap and looked white-faced.

'Darling, it's going to be fine, I promise. They're going to be a bit shocked at first, but after that they'll be OK. They love you very much. You know that, don't you?'

'What if it turns out that Paul's married?' Mia asked tremulously, as they pulled up outside her house.

Janine tensed. 'I'm sure he's not married. You'd have known, surely?'

'Well, he never wears a wedding ring and he certainly hasn't mentioned a wife, but I've never been back to his house. He's had the builders in putting in a new kitchen and he said it's in too much of a mess.'

Janine swallowed her unease and also the obvious question that sprung to mind. Where on earth had they found the privacy to get Mia into the predicament she was in? 'Stop second guessing things,' she soothed. 'Ready then?'

'Ready as I'll ever be,' Mia said, in a voice that was still wobbly.

As they walked up the path, Janine felt as if she were on her way to meet the firing squad, but that must be nothing to the way she guessed Mia felt. Especially as before she could even get her key out, the front door sprang open and Alison stood there, looking furious.

'You've got some explaining to do, young lady,' she yelled. And then before Janine could even open her mouth, Alison had dragged her daughter over the threshold and slammed the front door in her face.

For a moment Janine was so shocked she couldn't react. She could already hear raised voices the other side of the door. Perhaps she'd been wrong about the 'out of control' emotion. Should she ring the bell or do what every instinct urged her to do and disappear as fast as she could? The fear of facing Alison's wrath struggled with her conscience and her conscience won. She promised Mia that she'd support her and it was going to be pretty tricky to do that from out here. Summoning her courage, she rang the bell and waited.

Nothing. She tried again and then,

just as she was about to give up — after all, she couldn't actually force Alison to open the door — she heard movement from the other side. It opened a couple of inches and she saw her sister-in-law's tense, white face.

'If you've come to gloat because Mia told you before she came to us, then forget it,' Alison snapped.

'Of course I haven't come to gloat,' Janine said, stunned that Alison could think such a thing. 'She only came to me because she was so scared of telling you. It's sometimes easier to confide in someone who's not directly involved.'

'Well, we don't need your help.' Alison sounded as though she was close to breaking point and Janine struggled desperately to think of something that would let her know that she was on her side, that she was on both their sides. 'Look, I really don't want to interfere . . .'

'Then don't. I'm perfectly capable of taking care of my own daughter, thank you very much.'

The door was shut firmly once more, and this time Janine left it. Feeling shaky, but more with anger now than anything else, she went back to her car. She wasn't going to get anywhere by staying. Perhaps she could salvage what was left of the day and still go into work. Her boss had been none too happy when she'd phoned up and asked for an emergency day off, this morning. She would ring Nick later, she decided, once things had calmed down a bit. Her brother would understand that she'd only had Mia's best interests at heart. Or at least she hoped he would.

★ ★ ★

'So how did it go with Auntie Ali?' Kelly said, bouncing in from, school and helping herself to a chocolate biscuit and a can of cola from the fridge. 'Was she really mad? I bet she gave Mia hell, didn't she?'

'Don't fill yourself up on junk food.

You won't eat your tea,' Janine chided automatically.

'Yes, I will, I'm starving. And I'm only eating these to save you from temptation. Come on, Mum. What happened?'

'To be honest, I'm not really sure.'

'But I thought you were going to give Mia some moral support. You didn't chicken out, did you?'

'No, I did not chicken out.' She told Kelly what had happened.

'I always knew she was a bit of a psycho,' Kelly said, biting into another biscuit, her eyes widening.

'She is not a psycho. She was upset, that's all. I'd have been upset in her shoes. Now, can we just forget about it for now?' And she must have been sharper than she'd intended because Kelly didn't mention it again.

When she was sure her daughter was in bed, she phoned Nick.

He sounded strained and tired, which was very much what she'd expected.

'If there's anything I can do to help

— I mean it, Nick . . . ' She broke off, aware of how crass her words sounded. What on earth could she possibly do? She supposed she could offer to help them phone round and cancel some of the wedding arrangements, but she didn't like to suggest that. 'Is Ali all right?' she finished lamely. 'Shall I speak to her?'

'No, I think it's best that you leave it for now.' Nick lowered his voice. 'It'll all come out in the wash, I don't doubt, but best leave speaking to Ali for a while. She's taken it very badly.'

And that was the most he would say.

Janine hung up, feeling frustrated, but there was little else she could do. Families, she thought, going downstairs and giving in to the temptation to finish off the chocolate biscuits. She was past caring about her waistline. Chocolate was as comforting as a warm arm around her shoulders — but there were no warm arms in sight, so chocolate was going to have to do.

* * *

Pete knew that he would worry about Sarah discovering that bar of chocolate until dustbin day if he didn't get it out of the bin. He'd planned to wait until she'd left for work the next morning and then nip down and get it out to dispose of more permanently. But as he was lying in bed that night it struck him that Jean, next door, was probably under orders to keep an eye on him. The last thing he needed was her telling Sarah he'd been rummaging around in the wheelie bin. He'd be better off going to retrieve it under cover of darkness.

He waited until Sarah was snoring softly, then he slipped out of bed, fumbled around for his shoes and crept downstairs. Scared of waking Sarah, he hadn't bothered to dress, but it was a cold night and he didn't fancy wandering around outside in his underpants. He grabbed his coat from the hook by the front door, shivered as the cold lining made contact with his skin and let himself outside.

He hadn't thought to bring a torch, but fortunately there was plenty of moonlight. He leaned into the bin, which was half full of black bin-liners, screwing up his nose as the scent of three-day-old rubbish hit him. Theoretically, the chocolate bar should be on top where he'd left it, but he couldn't see it so it must have slid down the side. Thankful that he was tall enough to reach, he scrabbled around in the bottom of the bin. He touched something wet in one corner and then, bingo, he felt the unmistakable foil-wrapped squares beneath his fingers. Got it. He straightened up, closed the lid and glanced back up at the house, which was still in darkness. Phew!

He was just letting himself back in, the wrapper damp and slightly sticky with goodness-knew-what in his hands, when the hallway was suddenly flooded with light.

'Pete, what on earth are you doing?' Sarah was standing in the kitchen doorway in her dressing-gown, not looking in the slightest bit sleepy.

'Nothing,' he said, blinking rapidly and whipping the chocolate bar under his coat and knowing he must look the picture of guilt.

'I don't call wandering around outside at midnight with hardly anything on 'nothing'. What have you got under your coat?'

'Just my underpants,' he said, deliberately misunderstanding. Why did she have the knack of making him feel like a naughty schoolboy? He made to go past her, knowing that nothing on earth was going to induce him to confess.

She blocked his way. 'I saw you rummaging around in the dustbin. I was looking out of the window.'

'I thought you were asleep,' he said lamely, realising suddenly that she must have been faking it. She usually slept quite heavily.

'You woke me,' she muttered, and he could see a faint blush creeping up her neck.

'You thought I was sneaking down to the kitchen for a midnight snack, didn't you?' he said, deciding that attack might be the best form of defence.

'I wouldn't put it past you.' She went even redder and he knew he'd hit the nail right on the head. 'I mean, you haven't exactly lost much weight considering you've been on a diet for over a month.'

'Actually, I've lost more than a stone,' he gasped, the injustice of this remark hitting him like a punch in the guts. 'And you could try being a bit more supportive. It's not easy losing weight.'

'So you keep saying.' She made a lunge towards him and grabbed the front of his coat and, caught off guard, he wasn't quick enough to stop her. He hadn't thought to button it and now it swung back to reveal the bar of chocolate that he was holding tightly to his chest.

He looked down at it, noticing that the top wrapper was missing and so was some of the foil so that a lone square poked out of the top. A lone square that he saw, with sudden horror, had tooth marks in it. His eyes widened as he stared back at Sarah, and opened his mouth to protest that the tooth marks were nothing to do with him.

But she was already speaking, her voice threaded through with revulsion.

'You've been eating something out of the dustbin, haven't you? Good God, I didn't think that even you would stoop that low.' Her gaze flicked between him and the chocolate and he didn't answer her.

There was no need. Her eyes were as cold as chipped ice and he knew there was nothing, absolutely nothing he could say that was going to convince her that he wasn't guilty as charged.

3

"Three pounds off. Congratulations, Janine. That's very well done. Big clap, everybody, for Janine.'

Applause filled the room and Janine forced a smile and wished she felt as euphoric about her weight loss as their group leader apparently did. Perhaps if she hadn't been feeling so down about everything else, she would have been able to summon up a bit more enthusiasm. It had been six days since she'd dropped Mia back to her parents and, apart from the tense conversation she'd had with her brother, Nick, she'd heard nothing since.

She'd been existing on adrenaline so it was hardly surprising she'd lost weight, she thought ruefully, as everyone stopped clapping and she realised that their group leader had just asked her a question.

'So what's your secret, Janine?' she repeated. 'We're all dying to know.'

'Getting caught up in a good family crisis,' Janine said, hoping she didn't sound too cynical, and there was a ripple of nervous laughter as the group tried to work out if she was being serious.

And then, to her relief, Colette moved on to the next slimmer and the spotlight was no longer on her.

'Are you all right?' Pete asked her when Colette had rounded off by saying she hoped to see less of everyone at the next class. 'If you don't mind me saying, you look a bit tense.'

She glanced at his friendly, open face. The concern in his voice brought an ache to her throat and suddenly the thought of going home to an empty house — Kelly was at the pictures with her friends — was less than appealing.

'I've had a bad week,' she confessed. 'I wasn't joking about the domestic crisis. What I really need is to get away from it all for at least a month.'

'How about half an hour?' Pete said,

his dark eyes warm. 'I'm not rushing home — we could nip to the pub for a diet cola, if you fancy it?'

She smiled. 'Are you sure? I don't want to keep you from your wife.'

His eyes clouded briefly and she could have kicked herself for mentioning his wife. He'd only asked her for a friendly drink and she'd responded as if he'd made a pass at her. How tactless could you be?

'What I mean is . . . '

'No, it's all right.' He coughed. 'I know where you're coming from. To be honest, Janine, I'm pretty sure she won't miss me. But if you'd rather not?'

'I'd love to,' she said firmly. 'I know a great, little pub just round the corner. Do you want to follow me?'

They went in tandem to the Crooked Beams. It was odd walking through the ivy-covered main entrance with a man who wasn't Jonathan, she thought, as she headed automatically for the non-smoking section and propped her handbag on the bar.

'Small gin and tonic, please. What are you having, Pete?'

'I'm buying,' he said firmly.

He was actually quite a sweetie, she decided, as he turned from the bar and handed her a glass. 'Diet tonic. Is that OK?'

'Lovely. Thanks.' He had to duck his head under a beam as he steered her towards a table and she reflected that it was rather nice to be out with a man who made her feel small. Physically, as opposed to mentally, which had been Jonathan's speciality in the latter stages of their marriage.

'Penny for them?' he murmured.

'I was just thinking that I used to come in here with my husband. It was a long time ago, but it hasn't changed much.'

'Tell me to mind my own business if you like, but he wasn't anything to do with the domestic crisis, was he?'

'No. I only see him when he comes to pick up Kelly — she's our daughter. We split up just over a year ago.' She hooked the lemon slice out of her drink

54

and nibbled it, surprised that it didn't hurt more to discuss Jonathan.

'That can't have been easy,' Pete said gently.

'No, it wasn't at the time, but I'm over it now.' She met his dark eyes. 'It was probably for the best. Do you know that's the first time I've said that? At the time it was awful. I didn't think I'd ever get over it. He ran off with a younger woman, you see. Terrible blow to my ego, that was.' She smiled and added lightly, 'Especially as she was slim and beautiful.'

She half-expected Pete to come out with some platitude about that, which was what most of her friends had done when Jonathan had legged it, but he didn't. He just nodded sympathetically.

'But your domestic crisis was about something else?'

'Yes.' She told him about Mia and how her niece had come to her instead of confiding in her parents and how now her sister-in-law would no longer talk to her.

'I expect that's a bit of a pride thing,' he said thoughtfully. 'Especially as you hadn't been close before. She probably just needs a bit of time to get used to the idea. It can't be easy for her.'

'No,' she said, surprised at his sensitivity. 'Ali's the type of woman who can't cope when things don't go according to plan. I've always envied her a bit.'

'Perhaps she envies you, too. Things are rarely as perfect as they seem from the outside, are they?'

She smiled. 'No. Anyway, I'm being very selfish. Wittering on about my problems. How have you been doing? I take it you didn't have any more chocolate temptations, as I didn't hear from you again?'

He blinked at her a couple of times. 'No, you saved my life, thanks. If it wasn't for you, I'd have definitely put on weight this week.'

'And instead you lost five pounds. I still haven't quite worked out how you managed to do that.'

'Utter dedication,' he said, patting his

stomach modestly.

'Is your wife supportive? I bet she's really proud of you, isn't she?'

'It was Sarah's idea that I go on a diet, yes — mind you, she did have good reason.' He hesitated and Janine leaned forward in her chair.

'Well, come on, you can't leave it there.'

'No, no, I'm going to have to — it's too humiliating.'

'Oh, please.'

'OK, but I'm warning you — it's not pretty.' He screwed up his face in an exaggerated expression of horror. 'If you must know, the only reason I went on a diet in the first place was because Sarah told me she'd divorce me if I didn't lose four stone.' And then he smiled, so it was hard to tell how serious he was being. 'I wrote off her mother's dining-room chair, you see, when we went round for Sunday lunch. We'd just sat down for dinner and I was reaching for the salt and pepper and the damn thing just collapsed beneath me. I ended up on the floor with the chair in about five pieces. Gave the cat a hell of a fright, I can tell you. It was out of the door so fast you couldn't see its legs moving.'

'That would make a brilliant comedy sketch,' Janine said, biting her lip to stop herself laughing.

'It's not funny. You should have seen their faces. I thought Sarah's mother was going to have a coronary. She went this really strange colour, and Sarah was puffing and panting and yelling that I was making a fool of her.'

'It was probably a cheap chair. They don't make chairs like they used to.'

He snorted. 'No, it wasn't. But thank you for that vote of confidence.' He told her about the wheelie-bin incident, too, hamming it up so much that this time they both ended up laughing.

'You ought be a comedian,' she said, breathless.

'Yeah, I know. Can I get you another drink?'

'No, I'd better get back. But thanks

for tonight. You've really cheered me up.' She touched his arm lightly. 'Keep up the good work. It'll be worth it when you get to target. You'll have to go out and celebrate.'

'You're not doing so badly yourself — only another four pounds to go, isn't it? I'll miss you when you don't come to class any more.'

'Oh, I expect I'll still come along and get weighed. How else am I going to stay on track?'

He smiled again and she thought how attractive he was. His eyes were the colour of dark chocolate and his short, dark hair was a little spiky, but a spikiness that Janine suspected had more to do with a natural unruliness than any hair product. It wasn't just a looks thing — although she bet he'd be stunning when he reached the weight he wanted to be — it was his wry, self-deprecating humour. And his kindness. Sarah was a lucky girl.

'Good luck with your sister-in-law,' he said, as they went out to their respective cars. 'And if you ever feel the need to phone me for some extra motivation, don't hesitate.'

'Thanks, I won't. Ditto. And have a good week, Pete.'

★ ★ ★

Why did he have to joke about everything? Pete thought wryly, as he let himself into his empty house half an hour later. Why hadn't he just told Janine the truth? He headed for the kitchen and poured himself a stiff drink. The whisky tasted good after the insipid taste of diet fizz all evening. It burned down his throat in a fiery trail and warmed him and he refilled the glass.

Perhaps it was because he didn't want to face up to the truth himself, he thought ruefully, staring out of the kitchen window into the cold, starlit night and thinking about the row he'd had with Sarah over the chocolate. Not quite the slapstick comedy sketch he'd painted for Janine.

He could still see the disgust on Sarah's face as she'd stood at the end of their narrow hallway, her arms folded, her nose screwed up in utter revulsion. It had been that look that had told him exactly what she'd thought of him. And he'd known that he couldn't kid himself any longer. Standing in their hallway in the full glare of his wife's disgust, he knew that he'd been kidding himself. It didn't matter how hard he tried or what he did; it wasn't going to make a blind bit of difference. He might love Sarah, but he wasn't stupid. There was nothing he could do to change the simple fact that she no longer loved him.

And now she was gone. She hadn't even waited until the next day. She'd gone upstairs, packed an overnight bag and fled out into the night there and then as if she couldn't even bear to be under the same roof as him for one more second.

He'd pleaded with her to stay — to let him explain, even though he'd known it was useless.

'At least tell me where you're going to go,' he'd begged. 'You can't wake your parents up at this time of night.'

'I've no intention of waking Mum and Dad and you'd better not, either.' She stared at him, her face flushed — more flushed than it should have been, and the penny had suddenly dropped. How blind and stupid he'd been.

'This isn't about us, is it?' he whispered. 'There's someone else, isn't there? You're seeing someone else.'

She'd nodded. One brief little nod that had brought his world crashing down.

'Who is it?'

'It doesn't matter who it is.' She'd brushed past him and had opened the front door before he could move. 'I'll call you tomorrow, Pete.'

And like a coward he'd let her go, too shocked to stop her. What sort of a man did that? Let his wife go off to her lover without even knowing who it was. He'd stayed up all night torturing himself, and he'd been torturing himself pretty much all week. Knowing all the sordid details of Sarah's affair hadn't helped at all. It had just given him more to beat himself up with. She'd sounded relieved when she'd called him the next day. Relieved to tell him everything. How she'd fallen in love with her boss, Steve. Slick Steve, with his flash car and his flash haircut and his flash suits and his flash, flaming six-pack.

Pete poured himself another whisky and knocked it back in a couple of gulps. He knew all too well that his weight loss this week had more to do with hardly eating a thing than any kind of dedication on his part. He couldn't go on like this indefinitely, that was for sure, but his liquid diet was certainly working for now.

He looked at the whisky bottle and then shook his head — this was madness. He screwed the lid back on it, put it back in its place on the sideboard and headed wearily for bed.

★ ★ ★

Janine got home just before Kelly, but her attempts to look as if she'd been in for hours didn't fool her daughter for a minute.

'I went to the pub,' she confessed finally under Kelly's accusing gaze. 'I'm over eighteen. It's allowed.'

'Alone?' Kelly quizzed.

'No, I went with a few of the others.' Why had she lied?

'And was that Pete chap there?' Kelly's voice was ultra casual. 'Come on, Mum, you can tell me.'

'Yes, he was, but don't get any ideas. He's happily married.'

'Shame,' Kelly muttered, narrowing her eyes. 'You haven't looked so happy for ages.'

Janine escaped before Kelly could cross-question her any more. She'd have to be careful, she thought, as she got ready for bed. She might be over Jonathan, but the very last thing she wanted to do was to get between a husband and his wife. Thanks to Jonathan's dalliances, she knew exactly how that felt.

Over the next few days, she thought a lot about what Pete had said about Ali. Especially the bit about Ali being envious of her. Perhaps he was right, although she couldn't think why. Even if he wasn't, she decided that she ought to have another go at sorting things out with her sister-in-law. She'd have plenty of time this weekend because Kelly was seeing her father. But by Sunday evening, when she still hadn't done so much as pick up the phone to call Ali, Janine came to the uneasy conclusion that she was a coward.

Cross with herself, she ironed Kelly's school uniform for the next day and decided to pop round after work one evening that week. It didn't help that her weight seemed to have levelled out. According to the scales in the bathroom, she'd actually put on a bit since Tuesday, which was very unfair. The only treats she'd allowed herself this week had been a couple of chocolate biscuits on Wednesday; a tiny piece of low-fat Battenburg on Thursday, and half a packet of wine gums while she was watching a documentary on Friday. Hmm, maybe it wasn't quite so unfair. Perhaps she could work off some of the calories by going for a jog around the block.

She changed into her tracksuit bottoms, which felt reassuringly baggy, and an old top and was just pulling on her trainers when the front door banged and Kelly appeared with her overnight bag.

'Hello, love, you're early. I wasn't expecting you back for another couple of hours.'

'Dad and Sasha were going out for a meal so they decided to bring me back early. Dad said you'd be in.'

How typical of Jonathan to assume she'd have nothing better to do on a Sunday evening, Janine thought, with a twinge of irritation, but she let it pass. 'So did you have a good weekend? What have you been up to?'

'Oh, not much,' Kelly said, thumping her bag down in the hall. 'That's mostly washing. And I need my black jeans for tomorrow night, please, If that's OK?'

Janine felt another stab of irritation, but she suppressed this, too. It wasn't Kelly's fault that Jonathan's idea of looking after his daughter for the weekend didn't seem to include doing anything domestic.

'Go and put them in the machine. And anything else in that bag that's black.'

'Oh, and I need to talk to you about something,' Kelly called back over her shoulder. 'Have we got any crisps? I'm starving.'

So he hadn't bothered to feed his daughter either. Too busy going off for romantic meals with Sasha.

'No, I think they're all gone,' Janine said wearily. She seemed to remember eating the crisps, too. Maybe it wasn't quite such a surprise that she'd put on weight this week. 'Make yourself a sandwich. I'm just going for a jog.'

'What on earth for?'

'I'm trying to lose weight. Remember?'

'Which is why we don't seem to have any crisps left, I suppose,' Kelly shouted from the kitchen. 'Or biscuits. We haven't even got any bread, Mum. Have you been on a food binge or something?'

Janine sighed and abandoned the idea of jogging in favour of a trip to the express shop on the corner. When she got back, Kelly was sitting at the kitchen table reading the free newspaper and finishing off a cold can of baked beans.

'That is utterly disgusting,' Janine said, thumping the carrier bags of shopping down on the table. 'You could at least heat them up. What did you want to talk to me about?'

Kelly glanced up. 'Going to Florida. Dad and Sasha are going in October and they've asked me if I want to go with them.'

'For a holiday?' Janine asked, surprised. 'Well, I suppose you could if your father's paying. I'm not sure I can stretch to Florida at short notice. Flights to America don't come cheap.'

Kelly rested her fork across the empty bean can and put her chin in her hands. 'They're not just going for a holiday, Mum. Dad's company has offered him a job out there. It's a year's contract.'

Janine could feel the blood pounding in her head and for a moment she wasn't sure she'd heard right. 'A year?' she repeated faintly.

'Well, a year to start with. If it all goes well, I think they might stay out there permanently.'

'And he's asked you to go with him? Just like that? He didn't think to mention it to me?' Her legs felt suddenly weak and she sank into the chair opposite Kelly.

'I expect he thought he might as well ask me first. Because if I hadn't wanted to go then the whole thing would have been rhetorical anyway.' Kelly screwed up her eyes in consternation. 'I didn't mean to spring it on you.'

'And do you want to go?' Janine's palms felt damp and her mouth was very dry, and she wondered suddenly and irrationally if this was how Ali had felt when she'd found out that Mia was pregnant.

'I'm not sure, really.' Kelly frowned, her blue eyes thoughtful. 'The idea of living in another country sounds pretty cool. I'm not sure if I fancy living with Dad and Sasha, though. It's bad enough when I go round for weekends. They can't keep their hands . . . ' She broke off suddenly. 'Sorry, too much information.'

Janine blinked, acknowledging in some distant part of her mind the irony of Kelly wanting to spare her feelings when it came to Jonathan and Sasha's love-life, yet not having a clue about the death blows she was delivering with her casual announcement that she was considering living with her father in another country.

'Would you miss me then, Mum?' Kelly added, as though the possibility hadn't struck her before.

'Of course I'd miss you. You're my daughter.' Janine stood up abruptly, not wanting Kelly to see the sudden tears that had sprung to her eyes. She would kill Jonathan, she decided. Not content with breaking his vows and taking up with some bimbo who couldn't manage to put the washing-machine on, he now wanted to spirit Kelly away as well. She was torn between bursting into tears and pointing out a few home truths about Jonathan. If he couldn't look after their daughter properly for a weekend, how on earth would he cope full time? But pride stopped her. She'd always promised herself that she wouldn't let her feelings about Jonathan show in front of Kelly. He might not be her husband any more, but he was still Kelly's father.

'Are you all right, Mum?'

'Fine,' Janine lied, opening the carrier bags and putting away the shopping, on autopilot. But all she could think about was Kelly deciding to go to America. Fourteen was still young enough to absorb the change in culture and settle into a new school. Legally, she could probably stop her, but if Kelly did want to go, it would be very selfish of her to say she couldn't. Kelly would just end up resenting her and their relationship would be ruined anyway. She was in a no-win situation and Jonathan, as usual, held all the trump cards.

What if Kelly loved it there and decided never to come back? Her mind leaped ahead. What sort of relationship was she going to have with her daughter if she wasn't around to see her growing up, leaving school, taking exams and learning to drive? She'd have boyfriends that Janine would never meet. She might even end up marrying an American and Janine would be forced to watch her grandchildren growing up via pictures on the Internet. She swallowed a huge ache in her throat and forced calmness into her voice.

'When do you have to decide?'

'Oh, not for another week or so.' Kelly folded up the paper and looked at her mother and Janine could see mixed emotions in her eyes. Excitement at the prospect of living in another country and guilt because she hadn't thought about the implications.

'I'll have to have a proper think,' Kelly murmured. 'There's a lot to consider, isn't there?'

Janine nodded slowly, but inside she could feel a vice-like pain closing around her heart. And all she could think about was that this was going to be one of the longest weeks of her life.

4

When Janine woke up the next day the sun was bright and she could hear Kelly singing in the bathroom, but she felt as though a great, black cloud was hanging over her head. It would break her heart if Kelly chose to go and live in America with her father and his new girlfriend, but there was no way that Janine was going to let her daughter see how she felt. If Kelly chose to go, she would wish her every happiness and then she would go home and have a nervous breakdown in private.

'I'm going round Sharon's after school,' Kelly informed her as Janine dropped her off on her way to work. 'We're working on a history project together. So, don't worry about doing me any tea. Her mum said she'll do us something.'

'OK, darling.' Janine usually drove

straight off once she'd dropped Kelly off, but today she watched her walk through the school gates, tall and graceful and beautiful, her dark hair shiny in the sunlight. And she had to swallow an ache in her throat when she thought that these days might be numbered. That this simple journey that they made every day without even thinking about it might soon be just a poignant memory.

She'd always known, of course, that she'd have to let Kelly go one day. It was one of the hardest things a parent ever had to do. But she'd never imagined it would be like this. She'd never imagined that Jonathan could hurt her any more. She was tempted, very tempted, to go round and see him after work. But what was she going to say? She could hardly beg him not to take Kelly away. And even if she had, she doubted it would have made any difference. Jonathan always did what he wanted in the end.

The day seemed to drag on forever,

but at last it was over. She was about halfway home when she decided to go and see Ali. Her brother was never home before six so the two of them would have the chance to sit down and have a chat, woman to woman. That's if Ali let her in, of course. Her brother and sister-in-law were furious that Mia had told Janine about the pregnancy before talking to them.

Her heart was hammering as she pulled up outside the house, but she forced herself to walk up the drive and ring the bell. The worst that Ali could do was to slam the door in her face, and it couldn't be any worse than last time.

But Ali didn't slam the door. 'If you've come to see Nick, he isn't here,' she murmured.

'Actually, I came to see you, but if it's a bad time?'

'No, it's fine. Come in.'

She looked awful, Janine thought, with a tug of compassion. A pair of jeans and a crumpled T-shirt replaced her usual smart suit, her fair hair looked in need of a wash and she wasn't wearing make-up.

The house wasn't its usual immaculate self either, Janine saw as she followed Ali through to the kitchen. It was as though a cloak of sadness hung over everything.

Ali gestured her to sit down and she perched, uncomfortably, on a chrome stool at the breakfast bar, but before she could say anything, Ali said, 'I owe you an apology. I'm sorry for sounding off at you when you brought Mia back. My daughter's behaviour was hardly your fault.'

'It's all right. You were upset. I'd have been the same in your shoes.'

'No, you wouldn't. You'd have been nice and non-judgmental like you always are. I was a total cow.'

'I think you're being too hard on yourself. It must have been a terrible shock.'

Ali didn't say anything and, reluctant to let the silence stretch out for too long between them, Janine said gently, 'How

77

are things now? Any better?'

Ali shrugged her thin shoulders and then to Janine's horror she began to sob. Silent, aching sobs that shuddered her thin frame and brought every maternal instinct Janine had rushing to the surface. Unable to just sit and do nothing, she got up and went around the breakfast bar and rested a tentative hand on Ali's shoulder. 'Hey, love, don't upset yourself. I know it must seem awful now but it'll pass. It truly will.'

'You don't understand.' Ali sniffed noisily and rummaged in her bag for a hanky. 'You can't understand. You don't know all the facts.'

'Would it help to tell me? I want to help.' She waited until Ali had got herself back under control again, even though she thought it would have probably done her sister-in-law good to cry her heart out for a bit longer. She knew from experience that tears could be amazingly cathartic.

'Mia's disappeared.' Alison's voice was so soft that for a moment Janine wasn't sure she'd heard her right.

'She's left home. Gone off with that pervert boyfriend of hers. Three days ago, she just upped and left without a word.'

'Then how do you know she's with him?'

'He phoned to tell me. He had the temerity to suggest that he could look after my daughter better than I could. Do you believe that? It's his fault she's in this mess. She's only nineteen, but he's thirty-one. He should know better.'

'I couldn't agree with you more. Did he say where they were? Or what they planned to do?'

'I didn't give him the chance. I hung up on him.' Ali's mouth tightened, but Janine could see pain glittering in her tear-bright eyes. 'Nick said I was wrong to do that, but what else could I do? I couldn't bear to speak to him any more. Not after what he's done to my little girl. And now he's taken her away as well. I could kill him, Janine, I really could.'

'I'm not surprised,' Janine said with feeling. 'I'd feel exactly the same. It's a woman thing.'

'I was so sure you'd side with Nick and say I was overreacting.' She hesitated. 'I've always felt threatened by you.'

'What on earth for?'

'Because you have such a great relationship with Nick.' She sniffed. 'I'm an only child. I've never had a brother or sister. I guess I didn't like sharing him.'

Janine smiled wryly. 'I can understand that, believe me, and I know he's my brother, but I don't always agree with him. We used to fight like cat and dog when we were younger.' She touched Ali's hand. 'To be absolutely honest, I've always envied you a bit, too. Not because you were with Nick — I was happy for him — but because you're so beautiful. You always seem to wear the right clothes, have the right hairstyle. I feel like an old frump beside you.'

Ali looked genuinely amazed. 'That's

not beauty — it's hard work — and I suppose it's insecurity, too. I had it instilled in me from an early age that if I didn't always look my best I'd never keep my man.' She clapped her hand over her mouth and went scarlet. 'Oh, my God, I wasn't implying that you . . .'

Janine laughed. 'It's all right. I know you weren't. Anyway, I didn't put on weight until after Jonathan left me. He just fancied a younger model. And there's nothing we can do about that one, is there?'

Ali still looked stricken. 'I guess not.'

'So what happens when you try Mia's mobile?'

'She keeps it turned off.'

'And you don't know the number of his?'

'No. Nick was furious about that, too. But when he rang I was in too much of a state to think about practicalities. Did Mia give you any idea where he lived?'

'Only that it was the other side of town. She said he was her badminton instructor, though.'

'Yes, she told me that, too. I've tried phoning the sports centre, but he's on leave and they won't give me his home number. I feel so helpless, Janine. I feel as though I've lost my daughter and there's absolutely nothing I can do about it.'

'I understand exactly how you feel,' Janine said quietly, and then she told Alison about Kelly, and Jonathan's offer to take her to America.

'How on earth could he do that to you?' Ali sounded so genuinely horrified that Janine found herself smiling ruefully. 'To be honest, I doubt if he's given a second thought to how I feel. If he had he'd have said something to me before he mentioned it to Kelly. He's always been selfish.'

'But surely you can stop him. You've got full custody, haven't you?'

'Yes. But if Kelly wants to go and I stop her, she's never going to forgive me, is she? And I don't think I could live with that.'

Ali shook her head. 'Men — they

haven't a clue, have they? You must feel awful — and I've been going on and on about my problems. I'm so sorry.'

'Don't apologise. It hasn't happened yet. Maybe Kelly will decide not to go.' Not that there was much hope of that, Janine thought, remembering Kelly's hastily suppressed excitement. 'Anyway, there's nothing I can do about it until she's made up her mind. So let's talk about Mia. She can't keep her phone switched off forever. Why did she go off with this Paul bloke anyway? Did you have a row?'

Ali nodded miserably. 'That's all we've done since she told me. Looking back, I was too hard on her. I should have tried to understand things from her side, but I couldn't see past the fact that this bloke was so much older. And it wasn't much fun phoning round and cancelling all the wedding suppliers either. We'll be in debt for quite a while paying off that little lot.'

'What about insurance? Can you claim any of it back?'

'I don't think they pay out just because the bride changes her mind,' Ali said, raising her eyebrows. 'Still, I'm not worried about that too much. We were prepared for that. All I really want is the chance to apologise to Mia. I hate the thought of her being pregnant and not talking to me. Mad, isn't it?'

'No, love.' Janine touched Ali's arm. 'I'm really glad we've had this chat.'

'Me too.' Ali smiled for the first time. 'Do you remember when you told me about throwing all Jonathan's clothes out of the window that time?'

Janine nodded.

'And how I pretended to be horrified. Well, secretly I really admired you for doing it. I've never been able to let myself go to that extent. Nick says I'm too uptight.'

'No, you're not. You've just got more self-control than I have. I tell you what, though, it didn't half make me feel better.'

Now Ali laughed. 'I can imagine it would.'

And, as Janine smiled back at her sister-in-law, she knew that, at last, they'd sown the seeds of friendship. This hour of female solidarity would be the springboard for them to have a much closer relationship in the future.

* * *

'Congratulations, Pete, you are our slimmer of the week. Another four pounds off, making a grand total of two stone and three pounds. That is an amazing achievement.' Colette bent to stick a gold star into Pete's slimming record and he could smell her scent, Opium, which was what Sarah wore, and it was so evocative that he felt his heart leap into his throat and lodge painfully.

He clenched his fists in his lap and mumbled his thanks. Janine was sitting beside him and he was aware of her gaze, but he didn't meet her eyes because he knew he'd give himself away. He'd laughed his problems off when they'd been for a drink. He'd pretended he and Sarah were happy, but another fortnight alone had taken out the last of his reserves. He had to face the fact that his wife wasn't coming back. Sarah was happier than she'd ever been in her life, she'd informed him this week. And she'd seemed blissfully unaware that his despair was the cost of her happiness.

That was probably his fault, he mused, as he went out into the car park after class. He was too damn good at hiding his feelings beneath a veneer of humour.

'Pete, can I have a word?' Janine's voice broke into his thoughts and he realised guiltily that he'd totally ignored her since they'd left the class. He hadn't even offered his commiserations that she'd put on weight, which was the first time that had happened since they'd started the class.

'Sorry,' he said, turning and looking into her kind face. 'I was miles away.'

'Yes, I gathered that. Pete, tell me to

mind my own business if you like, but you look terrible. Have you had some bad news?'

He nodded, but couldn't bring himself to speak out here in the evening sunlight with the other slimmers calling out goodbyes and heading for their cars.

'Would a drink at the Crooked Beams be in order?' she asked softly, and then, as if sensing he was going to refuse, she added, 'I'm not taking no for an answer. Come on, ten minutes won't hurt you.'

He looked into her concerned, blue eyes and nodded. 'Yeah, go on then. If you're sure I'm not keeping you from something more exciting.'

'I'm sure.'

They sat at the same table as they had the first time and Janine looked at Pete's tired face and hoped she was doing the right thing. She'd resolved that they weren't going to do this again — it was how affairs began, wasn't it? Innocent drinks and the beginnings of friendship that turned week by week into something more. But his face looked almost haggard and, despite Colette's congratulations, Janine was worried. No one should lose so much weight so quickly. It wasn't healthy.

'What's happened?' she asked gently. 'If you'd rather not tell me then I'll understand, but I'm worried about you. Is it something you can talk to Sarah about?'

He shook his head and, to her shock, she saw that there were tears in his dark eyes. 'Sarah's left me. She's moved in with her boss. They've been having an affair for months, apparently. And muggins here was too stupid to notice.' He tried to force a smile, but it came out as a grimace and Janine felt desperately sorry for him.

'Listen to me, Pete. You are not stupid. There's no way you'd know if your partner doesn't want you to. Is it serious? Have you talked to Sarah — really talked, I mean?'

'She says he's her soulmate. The man

she's been searching for all her life. We've been married eight years and I didn't have a clue she wasn't happy. If I'd known I might have been able to do something.'

'And you might not,' Janine said gently. 'Not if that's how she feels. We can't make someone carry on loving us if they've decided they want someone else.'

He blinked and wiped his hand across his face. 'I'm sorry about this, Janine. I shouldn't be unloading all this stuff on you. I'm fine, really I am.' He held his hands out in front of him in a little gesture of casualness, which didn't quite come off because his fingers were shaking.

Janine wanted to take his hands and squeeze them. Well, what she really wanted to do was to get up and give him a big hug, but she was well aware that his barriers were as fragile as new ice and that it wouldn't take much to make him shatter.

'When was the last time you had

something proper to eat?' she asked briskly. 'In fact, when was the last time you had anything to eat?'

'I had toast this morning.'

'Anything since?'

'To be honest, Janine, I haven't been hungry.'

'If you don't eat you'll make yourself ill. Have you got any food in at home?'

He brushed a hand through his hair. 'There's plenty of bread — I'm hardly going to starve to death, Janine, look at me.' He patted his black corduroy trousers, which were baggy. The blue polo shirt he was wearing looked loose too.

'Have you looked in the mirror lately? Those trousers would fall down if you weren't wearing a belt.' She knocked back her drink and stood up. 'Come on, finish that. I'm taking you home.'

He looked startled.

'I live two minutes from here. I've got half a roast chicken in my fridge. Kelly's vegetarian so she won't eat it.

And I'm strictly on salads this week so it'll only go to waste. Humour me, Pete. Please.'

He came. He probably didn't have the strength to argue. He was as pale as ashes. She checked he was following her and, as they drove, she phoned Kelly on her hands-free phone.

'Where are you, darling?'

'Round Sharon's doing my history project. I told you.'

'I thought that was last night.'

'It's exam coursework. It's going to take weeks. How much weight did you lose?'

'I put on a pound.'

'Oh, bad luck, Mum. You'll have to stay off the crisps. Actually, I was about to call you. There's this documentary on about the Tudors later. That's the period we're working on. It would be really cool if we could watch it together. But it's quite late.'

'Can't you record it?'

'Yeah, we could, but Sharon's mum said I can stay over if it's OK with you.

Sharon's got a telly in her bedroom.'

After confirming that this was indeed OK, Janine put the phone down with mixed feelings. She wouldn't normally have agreed to a midweek stopover. But it was probably just as well in the circumstances. It would save the need for convoluted explanations.

Three quarters of an hour later they were seated in her lounge and, despite his protestation about not being hungry, Pete had eaten most of the chicken and some new potatoes and peas she'd heated up to go with it. She'd been worried she might feel awkward — she hadn't cooked for a man since Jonathan — but Pete was very relaxing company.

'I'm just trying to sabotage your diet, really,' she quipped, leaning back in her chair and looking at him with satisfaction. 'I'm not having you being slimmer of the week again. Not when I've done so abysmally badly.'

'You don't need to lose any weight anyway. You're lovely as you are.'

'Flattery will get you everywhere,' she

said, warmed, all the same, by the compliment.

'I mean it. I told you what I thought about stick insects. If you lose much more, you'll be in danger of turning into one.'

'Oh, you do say the sweetest things.' She took the tray from his lap. 'Would you like a coffee to wash that down?'

'If you're sure I'm not outstaying my welcome.'

'I'm quite sure.'

She washed up while she waited for the kettle to boil and when she took their mugs back in, Pete was asleep on the settee. He'd slipped sideways and he was breathing lightly and for a moment she stood looking at his face, which was peaceful at last. He must be exhausted, poor lamb. She bet he hadn't slept any better than he'd eaten for the last fortnight. Well, there was no way she was going to disturb him. She fetched the duvet from Kelly's bed. She half expected him to wake as she lifted his feet up on to the settee, which only just accommodated his six foot four frame, but he hardly stirred. She watched him for a few moments longer, then she covered him with the duvet, switched off the light and crept upstairs to bed.

When she came down in the morning, he was washing up.

'Janine, I'm really sorry. I didn't plan to hijack your settee — I must have been more tired than I thought.'

'If I'd minded I'd have woken you. Don't bother with that. I'll do it later. You'll make yourself late for work.'

'No, it's only fair that I make myself useful.'

She picked up a tea-towel and began to dry up. It felt totally natural to have him standing in her kitchen.

As he handed her the last fork, their fingers brushed and suddenly she was very aware of him. She glanced at him and he held her gaze for slightly too long. And she was sure he could feel it too. A little fizz of electricity that flared between them.

Flustered, she dropped the fork on the floor and they both bent to pick it up. When they stood up again they were almost touching. Janine took the final step. She put her arms around his waist and he didn't move away and, for a few seconds, she buried her face in his chest. He was wearing something citrus-scented and she breathed it in, emotions churning her stomach. It was a few seconds before she realised that the hug was one-sided. He hadn't reciprocated. And then she noticed that he couldn't have moved away if he'd wanted to because he was backed up against the fridge. Oh, Lord, she had a horrible feeling that she'd just made the biggest gaffe in history.

She raised her head to look at his face and saw that she was right. He looked stricken.

'Pete, I'm — so sorry. I . . . '

'Don't, Janine.'

They spoke at the same time and, as she snatched her hands from his waist, he put his up in front of him

— probably to ward off any further contact. But the result was that their hands sort of clashed mid air, the diamond ring her mother had left her knocking against his wedding ring.

He jumped as if he'd been stung. 'I'd better go,' he muttered, and all she could do was nod, her face hotter than a sauna on full blast.

The front door banged behind him, but she still couldn't move. She was usually quite intuitive. How on earth had she misinterpreted the situation so utterly? Mortified, she covered her burning cheeks with her hands. The one consolation — the only consolation — was that she'd never have to see him again because nothing on earth would induce her to show her face at the slimming club again.

5

Janine stared at the scales in horror. It couldn't be possible to put on a stone in a week — surely? But the evidence was there in front of her; the black digital figures of the slimming club scales never lied.

She glanced helplessly at the girl who had weighed her in.

'They're wrong, they must be. I haven't been perfect this week, but I can't have put on all that.'

The girl frowned and shook her head. 'They've been working OK until now.'

'Let me get off and get on again — please. Just in case.'

Janine sucked in her stomach as she stepped back on to the scales. Not that it was going to make any difference. This time when she glanced back at the reading they said something else. But it wasn't a read-out of her weight at all. She blinked and looked again, but they still said the same thing. *You Are A Fat Pig, Janine.*

It was at this point that she screamed and woke herself up. She was in bed and it was six forty-five on Wednesday morning — just before her alarm went off. Adrenaline was pounding through her and the sheets felt damp. She pushed them off and got up slowly. It had just been a nightmare, thank God. Probably guilt because she hadn't been to slimming club the previous evening. Or maybe it was a warning from her subconscious because she'd been comfort-eating all week. She hadn't put on a stone, though, she was sure about that. The bathroom scales confirmed that it was a pound. Not that she was particularly pleased about that. Why was it so incredibly difficult to lose weight and so effortless to put it back on again?

She sighed. The situation with Pete hadn't helped. She hadn't heard from him since she'd thrown herself at him.

Not that she'd expected to. He hadn't been able to get away quick enough. Her face still burned at the memory. She'd been worrying about Kelly, too. Her daughter had said nothing more about Florida. And neither had Janine, because if they didn't discuss it she could kid herself it wasn't real.

When she got downstairs, Kelly was at the kitchen table eating buttered toast. Janine reached for a slice absently, then decided to be strong, cut it in half and put the slice with most butter back on the plate.

'You're up early, love. Couldn't you sleep?'

'No. I was dreaming about Florida. Dad texted me last night to see if I'd had any more thoughts.'

'And have you?' Janine said, with forced nonchalance.

Kelly frowned and looked at her mother with unusual seriousness. 'How would you feel if I went? The truth, Mum, please. I need to know.'

'The most important thing to me is

that you're happy. It's a great opportunity.'

'That's not what I asked.' Kelly's blue eyes held hers. 'Would you be upset?'

'I'd miss you. Of course I would. And I expect I'd be upset for a little while. That's natural, isn't it?'

Kelly nodded slowly. 'I'd miss you a lot, too, but I'd really like to go.'

'Then you must,' Janine said, feeling a deep pain in her chest. 'America isn't the other side of the world. I can come and visit.'

'You hate flying.'

'I'd manage. And you could come back for holidays.'

Kelly smiled uncertainly. 'Do you really mean that? Wouldn't you be lonely?'

'Of course I wouldn't be lonely. If I didn't have you to look after I'd have a whale of a time. I'd join a few clubs, maybe a gym. I'd be young, free and single again.' How on earth was it possible for her voice to sound so light-hearted and carefree when this was her worst nightmare coming true? Lord, she'd rather put on ten stone than lose her beautiful daughter. She probably would, she thought, wondering why she couldn't seem to swallow the toast in her mouth. She'd be comfort-eating for the rest of her life. Kelly looked happier, though. She got up from the table and gathered up some brochures. Schools in Florida, Janine saw, feeling sick. When had Jonathan given her those?

'I'll phone Dad and tell him the good news then.'

Janine couldn't bear to answer this. 'Hurry up and get ready for school, love. I have to be in early.'

That wasn't true, but she needed to get out of the house. No, she was lying to herself. She needed to get away from Kelly before her thin façade of nonchalance crumbled. She didn't even think she could face work. She would drop Kelly at school and then phone in sick. Then, perhaps she'd drive to the

101

nearest cliff and hurl herself off.

By the time she'd dropped Kelly off, she'd decided she was being melo-dramatic. Her boss wouldn't be too impressed if she phoned in sick. They were too busy. And the nearest cliffs were fifty or so miles away; she probably didn't have enough petrol to get to them. This didn't stop the tears coming, though. They poured down her face as she waited at the traffic lights. She wiped them away with the back of her hand, glad of the unwritten law that prevents motorists staring too hard into other motorist's cars.

After work, she would call round and see Ali. She had a desperate urge to talk to someone and Ali would probably welcome the company; this Saturday would have been Mia's wedding day.

★ ★ ★

Pete dialled Janine's mobile, then disconnected before it could ring. Then he dialled it again and disconnected again. It was Wednesday evening, a week and a day since he'd seen her. The longer he left it, the harder it was going to be to get in touch. He cursed himself for being such a coward. Not just for now, but for last Wednesday. Why on earth had he fled like he had? He should have stayed and explained. Explained what, though? That every atom of his body had yearned to kiss her, to hold her tight in his arms, to bury himself in her warmth. That the strength of his feelings had shocked him because he still loved Sarah, didn't he? Every time he'd tried to conjure up his wife's face, he'd found himself looking into Janine's blue eyes instead.

Janine had haunted his dreams all week, the scene in her kitchen replaying a thousand times, but he always woke before he could touch her. Woke up to a cold, empty bed and the aching realisation that he'd never see her again if he didn't do something about it. He'd clung to the fact that at least he'd see her at slimming club, but she hadn't shown up last night.

'Poor woman's got flu,' Colette had said when he'd enquired about Janine's whereabouts. 'You don't look too well yourself, Pete. You're not coming down with it, too, are you? There's a lot of it around.'

'Could be,' he'd muttered, knowing full well that his pallor had nothing to do with flu and everything to do with the amount of whisky he'd been consuming. He wondered how long it took to become an alcoholic. Could it be done in four weeks? Four and a half, maybe. He checked the whisky bottle on the sideboard. Almost empty and he'd only bought it at the weekend. Making a decision, he poured the remainder of the bottle down the sink to prove he wasn't an alcoholic. It felt good. Proved that at least he had control over something in his life.

He glanced at the clock. Just after seven. He wasn't going to get much more work done today. And having decided he wasn't going to spend another evening drinking his way into a state of miserable numbness, he was restless.

Perhaps it would be easier to go and see Janine. He was pretty sure she didn't have flu, but if she did, then at least he could offer to get her in some shopping or something. Grabbing his car keys and checking in the hall mirror to make sure he looked halfway presentable, he left the house before he could change his mind.

★ ★ ★

Ali had taken one look at Janine's face and then given her a hug, and the hug had unravelled Janine completely. She'd cried on her sister-in-law's shoulder; noisy, abandoned tears that she couldn't hold back and which had made her feel marginally better.

Now it was an hour later and they were sitting in Ali's kitchen having consumed several mugs of tea and half a fruitcake.

'Maybe Jonathan will change his mind,' Ali said. 'I mean, he's never been a hands-on father, has he?'

'I don't think he will. We're meeting up on Friday for a chat. He says it's a fantastic opportunity for Kelly, and I know he's right but that doesn't help. Anyway, enough of my problems. What's happening with Mia?'

'Well, we've just eaten what was destined to be the top of her wedding cake,' Ali said, with a slightly wry smile. 'As we'd already paid for it; I thought we might as well enjoy it.'

Janine nodded, knowing that if she could smile about it, even ironically, Ali had come a long way.

'And have you spoken to Mia?'

'Yes. You were right; she couldn't keep her mobile off forever. I caught her and I apologised for the things I'd said and I told her how much I loved her, and, well, the upshot was that we met Paul last night.'

'Blimey,' Janine murmured. 'And is he still in one piece?'

'Yes — you're never going to believe this, but I quite like him, Janine. He was as nervous as anything. Kept apologising. Said he knew we probably hated his guts, but that he really did love Mia and that he wanted to be with her and look after her, and he hoped that one day they'd end up getting married.'

'Wow. What did Nick say?'

'He took a little more talking round — you know Nick — but he was all right eventually. They even shook hands. Paul's just had his house done up and he and Mia are living there. We're going round at the weekend.'

'So all's well that ends well,' Janine said thoughtfully, trying to remember how many slices of fruit cake she'd had. 'Apart from poor Carl, I suppose.'

'Yes, poor lad. I don't suppose his parents will ever talk to us again, but I can see why Mia had her head turned — if that's not too old-fashioned an expression. And that's something I never thought I'd say.' She hesitated.

'I wish things could work out as well for you.'

And then the front door banged and Nick breezed into the kitchen.

'Hi, girls. Eating all my hard-earned money, I see.'

'Not for much longer,' Janine said, standing up and giving her brother a hug. 'I'm about to go and pick up my daughter from her friend's.'

* * *

Pete wondered whether he should try just one more time. Having psyched himself up to talk to Janine, it had been a disappointment to find she wasn't in. And now he didn't want to leave before he'd seen her. But if he drove round the block too many more times he'd get picked up for kerb crawling. Perhaps she'd gone out for the evening. He glanced back at the house, just in case by some remote chance she'd sneaked in without him seeing. But all looked exactly as before. This was ridiculous.

He would simply have to come back tomorrow. Sighing, he indicated to pull out, just as a car turned into the road.

His heart began to race as Janine's familiar blue Escort came into view and she parked outside her house. With fingers that trembled slightly, he switched off the ignition. He almost changed his mind when he saw that Janine wasn't alone, but if he didn't do it now, he'd never have the nerve to come back again.

Locking his car and stuffing the keys in his pocket, he headed across the road.

'Janine. Have you got a minute?'

She hesitated, but it was an age before she turned towards him, and he wondered if she'd had to compose her face because she looked at him almost blankly. She'd been crying, he thought with a little jolt. Not over him, surely. 'Don't flatter yourself, mate,' taunted his inner voice. 'She's far too beautiful to spend any time worrying about an idiot like you.'

'Hello, Pete.' Her voice was blank,

too, but Kelly was staring at him with open curiosity. 'What can I do for you?'

Heck, this was even worse than he'd envisaged. All his carefully rehearsed words dried in his throat and he could only stare at her helplessly.

Kelly's bright voice filled the space between them. 'I'll go in, Mum, shall I? I've got loads of homework to do. Upstairs,' she added emphatically, and disappeared into the house.

Pete cleared his throat, feeling hot and uncomfortable in the balmy, summer evening. 'I just wanted to — er — apologise for last week. And I wanted to make sure you were OK. Can I come in?'

'Sure, if you think it's going to help. But I rather thought it was me who should be apologising.'

As he followed her along her hallway, she called back over her shoulder, 'Unless you're apologising for turning me down. But that's hardly necessary. I'm sorry I misread the situation. I'm out of practice.'

Then they were standing in her lounge, facing each other, a metre or so apart. He cleared his throat. 'You didn't misread the situation. That's what I wanted to talk to you about.'

Something flickered in her eyes. She looked so vulnerable, so uncertain of herself, and he yearned to hold her, but he had to get this right. He wasn't going to get another chance.

'Janine, I panicked. That's all.'

'I didn't realise I was so scary,' she said, but her lips twitched.

'You're not. You're the loveliest woman I've ever met. Not just because of how you look, but because of how you are.'

'Pete, stop it. Pu-leez.' And this time she did smile. 'I don't need to be let down gently. I'm a lot tougher than I look. How did slimming club go? You look as if you've lost some more.'

He frowned. This wasn't going according to plan at all. 'I didn't come round here to talk about slimming,' he said, crossing the gap between them in two swift strides and putting his arms around her. She stared up at him, shock in her blue eyes, but before she could speak, he cupped her face in his hands and kissed her, very tenderly and very thoroughly. Just so there could be no mistake, no confusion about the sort of kiss it was. The sort that transcended friendship utterly — in one long, breathtaking, shuddering moment.

And, to his immense satisfaction she seemed to be in no more of a hurry to end it than he did.

A wolf-whistle brought them back to reality. 'Sorry to interrupt,' Kelly said, standing with her hands on her hips in the doorway. 'I need that book on the table. But if you're going to snog someone's face off in the lounge, Mum, you could at least introduce me.'

The introductions, immediately followed by the explanations, took some time. Partly because Janine had forgotten she'd told Kelly that Pete was happily married.

While she explained, Pete sat on the

settee beside her, holding her hand as if he couldn't bear to let it go. Sitting next to him was like being an inch away from a force field. And yet, paradoxically, it was also amazingly comfortable. Janine couldn't make up her mind whether she wanted to tear all his clothes off — probably wouldn't take much effort, they were hanging off him anyway — or just curl up and go to sleep in his arms. She kept having to resist the urge to lay her head on his shoulder, but finally Kelly's curiosity was satisfied and she went up to bed.

And, still holding hands, she and Pete stayed on the settee and talked about Sarah.

'Rebound relationships aren't a very good idea,' Janine said quietly. 'You've been very hurt. Maybe you should spend some time healing. Get yourself sorted out emotionally before you dash into something new.'

'In normal circumstances I'd agree with you.' His dark chocolate eyes held hers. 'But the truth is, Janine, it was over between Sarah and I long ago. I just didn't want to face up to the fact that we were finished. Emotionally, it's been dead for years.'

'Are you sure?'

'Oh, yes. I nearly drank myself into an early grave trying to get you out of my head, but I can't. I want to be with you.' He kissed her again and left her in no doubt that he meant it. But then, rather to her disappointment, he drew gently away. 'It's nearly midnight. I'd better make tracks.'

'It's far too late to drive home. Why don't you stay here?'

He smiled. 'Thanks, but I'm not sure I could face another night on your sofa.'

'Who said anything about you sleeping on the sofa?'

'What about Kelly?' he said anxiously.

'Kelly will be fine, but if you're worried you can sneak out at the crack of dawn.'

And he did, which was why it was such a shock to go past Kelly's bedroom on her way to the bathroom the next morning and hear her crying her heart out.

Guilt scrambled Janine's stomach as she pushed open her daughter's door. 'Darling, whatever's wrong?' She was across the room in a stride. 'Have I upset you?'

Kelly shook her head. 'No, it's me. I'm so sorry, Mum, but I've thought and thought about it and I've decided I can't go to Florida.'

'Why?' Janine asked, her heart jamming in her throat.

'Because I'm happy here. All my friends are here, and you're here, and I want to see Mia's baby when it's born and this is my home. I'm really sorry, Mum. I know you wanted me to go, but I just can't.'

'I didn't want you to go. What on earth made you think that?'

'You said it,' Kelly said, sniffing. 'You said if you didn't have to look after me, you'd have a whale of a time.'

'I wasn't telling the truth,' Janine

said, feeling a great bubble of happiness rising. 'I just didn't want to stand in your way.'

Kelly's eyes widened. 'You sounded pretty convincing.'

'Oh, darling. I've been dreading you going.' She hugged Kelly so hard neither of them could breathe. 'That is the best news in the world. Are you really sure?'

Kelly nodded. 'I've never got on with Sasha very well, to be honest. She's too much of a fake.' She narrowed her eyes. 'I like Pete, though. He's nice. It's serious between you two, Isn't it?'

'I think it might be. Do you mind?'

'No, of course not. And I'm not just saying that so I don't stand in your way.' She raised her eyebrows and gave a rueful grin. 'I'm not as unselfish as you, Mum. And I'm not deaf either, so tell him if he's going to sneak out first thing in the morning, he ought to push his car up the road a bit further before he starts it!'

Janine wouldn't have gone to slimming club the following Tuesday if Pete hadn't made her. She was still arguing as they queued up to be weighed.

'I've put on loads. I know I have. This is going to be so humiliating.'

'Three pounds off,' announced the same girl who'd weighed her in her nightmare. 'Congratulations, Janine. Only another couple of pounds to target.'

Amazed, she waited for Pete to join her in their usual seats. 'I can't think how that happened. How did you get on?'

'Four pounds,' he said smugly. 'But I had a lot more to lose than you. I'm way off my target weight.'

'I'm not so sure about that. Did Colette set that weight for you?'

'No, I set it myself.'

'It wasn't, by any chance, based on something Sarah said, was it?'

He nodded.

'Well, I think she's wrong. You look fine to me. And I'd say I'm in quite a good position to judge.'

To her delight, he blushed at the innuendo. He was such a sweetie. So gentle and kind and so unaware of how attractive he was.

And then Colette started the class and Janine went into dream mode, until she heard their leader's voice.

'Congratulations, Pete. Another amazing achievement. Are you going to give us a clue as to how you did it?' She was standing in the middle of the room, a smile on her face, her immaculate eyebrows raised enquiringly.

'He can't tell you,' Janine heard herself saying, as she reached for Pete's hand. 'Because he's far too much of a gentleman.'

'I'm going to kill you,' Pete hissed, as the entire class cheered, but he was smiling broadly and he kissed her fingers, which got them another round of applause.

'Moving swiftly on,' said Colette, but she was laughing, too.

And Janine thought about the first

time she'd set eyes on Pete, looking as nervous as a schoolboy and twice as vulnerable.

'Penny for them,' he murmured, as they went out into the sultry, August evening a few minutes later.

'I was thinking something very silly. You'll laugh.'

'I promise I won't.'

'OK — well, I was just thinking that a slimming club isn't the most obvious place for a romance to begin. So I was wondering if it was all the talk of targets that attracted Cupid.'

He looked puzzled and Janine giggled. 'I told you it was silly. Ignore me.'

'You are impossible to ignore,' he said, his dark eyes softening. 'Ouch.'

'What?' Janine asked, alarmed, because now he was rubbing his chest with a pained expression on his face.

'I think the little beggar just got me with one of his arrows. Straight through the heart.' And then he put his arms around her and whispered into her hair, 'Right on target.'

We do hope that you have enjoyed reading this large print book.

Did you know that all of our titles are available for purchase?

We publish a wide range of high quality large print books including:
**Romances, Mysteries, Classics
General Fiction
Non Fiction and Westerns**

Special interest titles available in large print are:
**The Little Oxford Dictionary
Music Book, Song Book
Hymn Book, Service Book**

Also available from us courtesy of Oxford University Press:
**Young Readers' Dictionary
(large print edition)
Young Readers' Thesaurus
(large print edition)**

For further information or a free brochure, please contact us at:
**Ulverscroft Large Print Books Ltd.,
The Green, Bradgate Road, Anstey,
Leicester, LE7 7FU, England.
Tel:** (00 44) **0116 236 4325
Fax:** (00 44) **0116 234 0205**